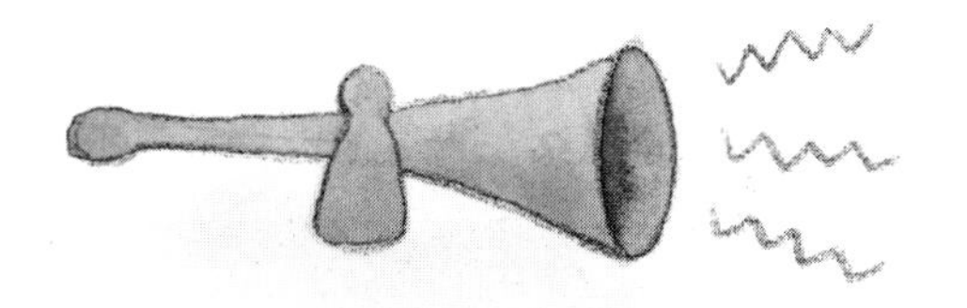

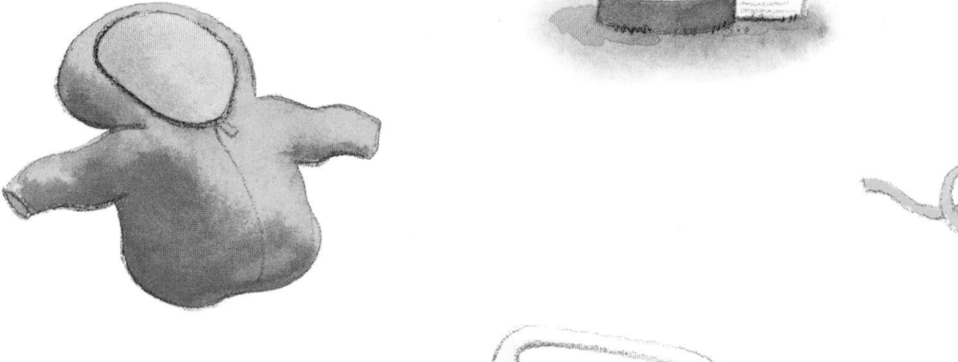

JULIANNA B.
OCEAN BAY, U.S.A.

FERRY

BOAT RIDE!

by Anne Rockwell

illustrated by Maggie Smith

CROWN PUBLISHERS New York

Our summer island is way out at sea—
too far for any bridge to cross.
That's why we take the ferry there.

Ferry Terminal

“I’ll meet you up in the bow,” my father says
as he waits his turn to back our car onto the ferry.
Bow is what you call the front of the boat.
Stern is what you call the back.

Lots of people come aboard
bringing bicycles and backpacks,
totes and duffels and coolers.
A forklift brings heavy cartons aboard.

We climb the port stairs to the upper deck.
Port is the left side of a boat, and *starboard* is the right.
Our ferry is named the *Julianna B.*
Boats are always called "she"—I don't know why.
We watch as the last car drives aboard.
Then the gate is shut across the ramp.

I hear the *Julianna B.*'s engine
start to rumble.
I feel it throbbing below the deck.
Water around the ferry swirls
in circles.

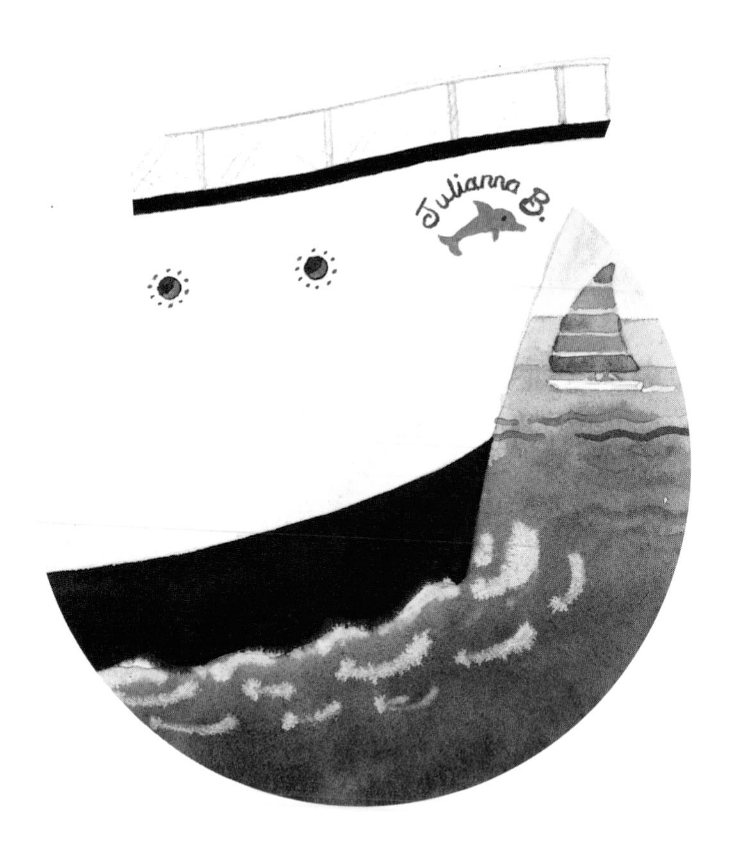

The captain blasts the whistle.

A baby starts to cry when he hears that noise.
That baby's so little,
I'll bet he's never been on the ferry before.
But I have.

I've heard the captain give three blasts of the whistle
announcing we're leaving the harbor
every single summer since I was born.

We decide to sit on the upper deck and my father finds us.
Now we're under way.
I stand at the starboard rail and watch
as the captain steers the ferry carefully out of the harbor.
Little sailboats are sailing in the cove.

LIFE
LIFE
Julianna

The lighthouse at the end of the long point is flashing.
I put on my windbreaker and zip it up tight.
The waves are bigger, for now we're out at sea.
The triangular bow cuts through the water,
turning it white and frothy.
I wish I could see a whale.
My mother says that she once did.
It was swimming alongside the ferry
when she was a little girl.

But suddenly I can't see anything.
The horizon between sea and sky is gone.
Our ferry is wrapped in gray and fuzzy fog.
Sea spray drips from the rail.
The foghorn sounds, and somewhere another boat
sounds her foghorn, too.
Another does, and then another.
There must be lots of boats out there,
but I can't see a single one.

The radar antenna above the pilot house turns around and around,
telling our captain when other boats are near.
The ferry rises and falls with the waves
while the foghorn blows and blows.

But now no foghorn answers us.
We're all alone in this part of the sea.
A wake of white water races alongside the ferry,
and I hear the loud swish of the waves.

Julianna

Our foghorn goes on blowing, and from somewhere
I finally hear a lone foghorn answer—
a long, deep, muffled sound—a voice like fog.
Suddenly I see a smudge of white and a gleam of yellow.
A lobster boat piled with traps looms out of the gray.
People on deck wear bright yellow aprons.
The boat wallows in the waves, drops a trap, then turns,
trailing a long white wake of water.

BAY, U.S.A.
JULIANNA
STS

Soon something shimmers in the gray water below me.
No! It can't be!
It's much too small to be a whale.
I think it must be a school of little shiny silver fish.
But it's not. It's sunshine!
Just like that, the fog is gone.
Far in the distance, I see something.
"Look! Do you see it way off there?"
I point toward the horizon.
Everyone comes to the rail to look.
Our summer island rises from the blue and sparkling sea.

Seagulls soar into the sunlight,
squealing and mewing alongside the ferry.
I toss a pretzel over the rail.
One smart seagull catches it in midair.

A big red buoy to starboard rises and falls
with the waves and the wake of the boat,
clanging its bell as it rocks.
I can see seaweed and mussels and barnacles
clinging below the buoy's dark water line.
Lots of things live hidden beneath the water—
even the whale I didn't see.
The red buoy tells the captain we're entering
the narrow channel that leads to the island's harbor.

The engine grows quieter as the *Julianna B.* slows down.
Soon I can make out the beach where we swim,
the old hotel where weekenders stay,
and the lighthouse high on the bluff.

From the port side, I see a bright green light
at the end of the jetty.
People fishing from the jetty wave to us.
The captain blasts the whistle
to tell the harbormaster that we're going to dock.

Then the ferry stops.
For a moment she is still and quiet
while the water twirls around and around.
Then the engine rumbles and roars again,
and the *Julianna B.* turns all the way around.
A ramp comes down with a clang,
and our stern lurches up to it.

The engine stops—for good, this time.
Everything is quiet, except for the people on shore
calling to passengers on board the ferry.

The crew tosses huge loops of rope
around tall pilings rising from the water.
Now the ferryboat is secured to shore.
A seagull heads straight for the clam shack
with the red and white awning
that's up the hill from the parking lot.

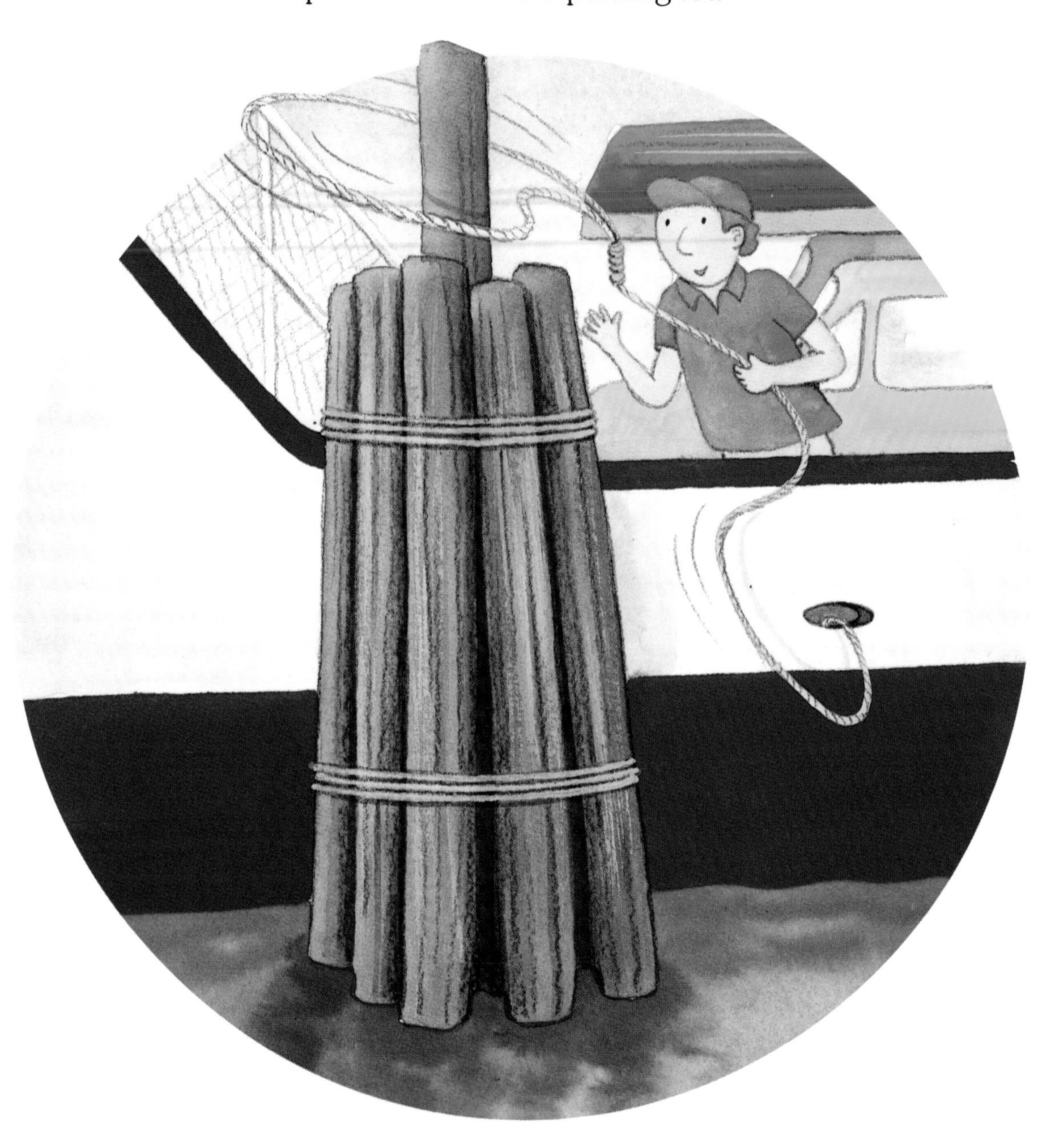

My father goes below deck to where the cars are.
My mother and I watch them drive off the ferry.
As soon as the very last car
has bumped and rolled over and off the ramp,
all the passengers go down the stairs.

They take bicycles, backpacks, duffels, coolers, and totes ashore with them.

The *Julianna B.* is empty now.
Our ferry looks very big in the little harbor.

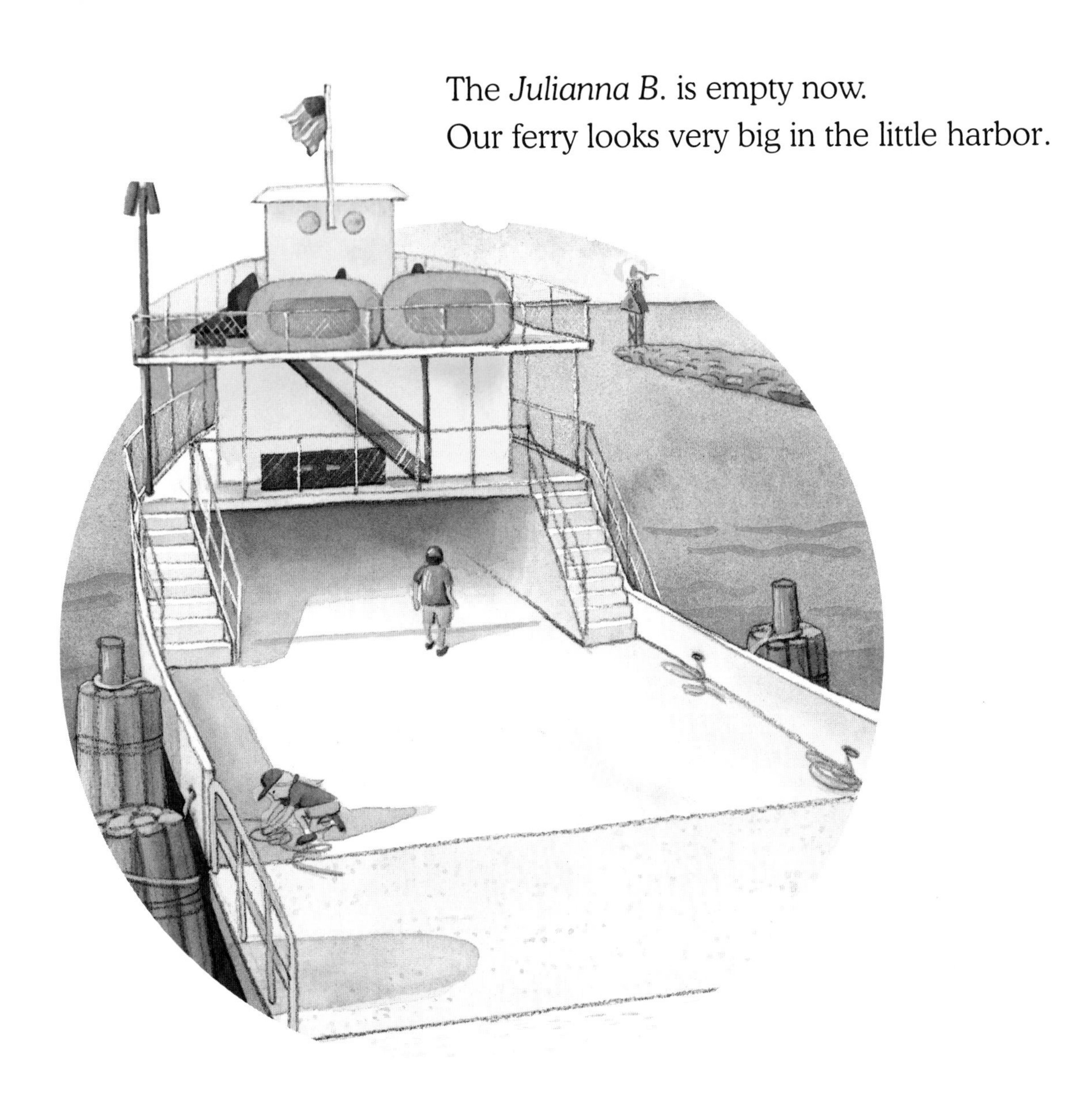

I sniff the island air.
I love the way it smells—part like the sea
and part like gardens that grow on land.

"Salt air always makes me hungry," my father says
as soon as my mother and I get into the car.
"How about you?
Shall we stop for some clamcakes
before we go to the cottage?"
"Yes!" we say.
So that's exactly what we do.

For Nigel—A.R.
For Caroline Murphy—M.S.

Published by Crown Publishers, Inc., a Random House company,
201 East 50th Street, New York, NY 10022

CROWN is a trademark of Crown Publishers, Inc.
www.randomhouse.com/kids
Printed in the United States of America

Library of Congress Cataloging-in-Publication Data
Rockwell, Anne F.
Ferryboat ride! / by Anne Rockwell ; illustrated by Maggie Smith.
p. cm.
Summary: A little girl notices all the sights, smells, and sounds along the way when her
family takes a ferryboat to their summer island.
[1. Ferries—Fiction. 2. Islands—Fiction.] I. Smith, Maggie, 1965- ill. II. Title.
PZ7.R5943Fe 1999
[E]—dc21 98-28827
ISBN 0-517-70959-7 (trade)
ISBN 0-517-70960-0 (lib. bdg.)

10 9 8 7 6 5 4 3 2 1
First Edition